AMAZING GRACE

Tre Chado

Amazing Grace: Bloodline of the Tide 2 follows Grace, a young woman who returns to her ancestral village after the death of her mother, Helen—a woman once whispered about in fear and reverence. What begins as a quiet mourning turns into a spiritual awakening when Grace uncovers a hidden hymn, an ancient spiral, and a forgotten language of freedom. As the land begins to respond to her voice, the past refuses to stay buried—bones remember, the wind listens, and the ancestors rise to be named. Caught between those who fear her power and those who need it, Grace must decide whether to silence the truth or become its keeper. Blending folklore, memory, and spiritual realism, *Amazing Grace* is a story of inheritance, identity, and the sacred responsibility of giving voice to what was never meant to be forgotten.

DEDICATION

To the daughters of dust and rivers.
To the ones whose names weren't given,
who still found a way to sing.
This is for you.

COPYRIGHT

CHAPTER LIST:

Chapter 1: Grace Notes

Chapter 2: The Lost Hymn

Chapter 3: Soil And Spirit

Chapter 4: Where The Wind Spirit Stop Singing

Chapter 5: Names That Weren't Given

Chapter 6: Rivers Of Bones

Chapter 7: The Ash And The Answer

Chapter 8: The Blood That Sang

Chapter 9: The Spiral Uncoils

CHAPTER 1: GRACE NOTES

The breeze carried the scent of yam skins and hibiscus petals, threading through the hillsides like a hymn remembered only by the wind. It slipped past the broken gate, skimmed the rusting roof, and into the houses left by those who had turned into memories of dust. Grace sat barefoot on packed red earth, skirt pooling around her legs like a forgotten blessing. Her fingers curled into the weeds, searching for a pulse beneath the soil.

Seven days since she returned.

Fourteen since Helen's burial.

Twenty-one since the seashore last breathed her name.

Time fell slowly, like sand in an hourglass; its hush echoed beneath her ribs—low, steady, patient. It reminded her of how Helen used to pause mid-sentence as if listening to something beneath the waves. That silence always unnerved Grace. Now she understood. It was reverence, not fear, and the tide was listening again.

This wasn't grief, not really. Grief was sharp. This was something slower, stranger—like the way the sound of silence changes its shape depending on the listener.

The sun had reached its peak, and the cicadas had only just emerged, gossiping in the trees. Grace closed her eyes and listened not for sound, but for presence. She understood that silence could speak if you let it. In that abyss she felt the past stir—not just Helen, but the others too. Those who walked crooked passages, the long way from spirit to dust.

Helen always said, "There are songs the living cannot sing, unless they have walked barefoot across the soul of the ocean."

Back then, Grace had rolled her eyes—too modern, too logical. Now she was not so sure.

The house on the beach was a song in itself. Every creak, every loose nail, every warped shutter was part of a larger chorus. The walls were thick with age, layered with ochre paint that sustained generations of secrets. Grace had spent most of her childhood trying to escape this place, only now to feel its pull like gravity.

Her bare heel, crescent arch, brushed against something beneath the porch steps—an old, rusted spoon, bent like a waning moon. She picked it up. It was Helen's. Helen used to use it to stir her oils, not her porridge.

Tools mattered.

Intention mattered.

Grace whispered, "It must be a sign," then slipped it into her skirt pocket.

Inside the house, it still smelled like calendula and bay leaf. Everything remained where Helen had left it, even the dried starfruit slices hanging in the kitchen window, catching the morning light like sun-kissed prayers. On the mantle stood stones stacked in odd formations, resembling unbalanced rituals. Helen always said they were there to catch bad luck in the cracks of the in-between. Grace turned and left, heading to the attached back house.

Charisse was humming when Grace entered. Her voice was low and tired as she cut okra, her fingers sticky with its sap. She glanced over at Grace, then back to the cutting board. Grace had aged. Even Charisse could see it now, though she would never reveal it outright; the lines on Grace's face were deeper than she remembered. Neither Father Time nor Mother Nature had been kind to her. There was no more pretending—the careless young girl had left.

"You were out there long," Charisse said without looking up, focused on the blade.

"I was listening," Grace replied.

"To what?" Charisse clicked her tongue. "Has the sand said something to you now?"

"It confided in me," Grace said. "What it remembers."

Charisse sighed softly. "You talk like Helen more every day."

Grace didn't respond. The truth clung like thick humidity—inescapable and best left undisturbed.

Grace's return had been unannounced. The funeral had drawn people from as far as Guyana and St. Lucia, not because Helen was popular, but because she was known. Loved? No. Feared? Doubtful. Even the priest stumbled through her eulogy, carefully choosing words like mystical and enigmatic, avoiding anything too spiritual or supernatural, as if he were afraid to offend the unknown.

People accused Helen of many things: witchcraft, healing, seduction, and isolation. You name it, somehow it was tied to Helen. But no one accused her of being small.

Grace had only meant to stay a few days after the burial—long enough to grieve politely, to nod at old faces that she barely remembered. The village had changed, and she had changed even more. The pace was slower here; the clocks weren't digital. Stories weren't told in text, and streetlights did not interrupt the night stars.

She had forgotten how dark true dark could be, and how loud her thoughts became without the city's noise drowning them out.

That night, after supper, Grace wandered through the house. Her feet carried her past the parlor with its cracked leather chair and dusty piano, down the hallway lined with family photos—some blurred, others scratched by time—until she reached a closed room marked by a posted sign: Helen's Sanctuary.

She stood at the threshold for a long time, remembering the two years she had lost.

The air was different here, thicker. Something about it felt set apart. The room had not been disturbed. It felt wrong to contaminate it by letting the outside air in.

The altar near the window was still intact. Bottles of oil lined the wooden shelf—tallow, extra-virgin olive oil, coconut oil, palm oil, castor oil, and mango butter. There was also something darker, something elusive that she could not name.

She turned to the dried herbs that hung upside down like sleeping birds. Books were not stacked by topic but by energy, some bound in leather, others wrapped in old banana husks. They were all old books, given to Grace from her grandmother before she crossed into the unseen with Abel in grasp.

On the floor sat a woven mat, half-tattered, constructed like a spiral.

Grace stepped forward, kneeling beside it. Her fingers brushed a book. Its cover was frayed like cloth, but still intact. She opened it carefully. Inside were pages of the strange music—a kind of melodic spellwork. The symbols were half-rune and half-word, and the lines of the song, written in no language she'd been taught yet, made the melody ring familiar.

She had heard it in her dreams.

A chill traced her spine. This was no coincidence. This was a summons.

She sat on the mat in a trance, legs folded. The book rested on her lap, like a sleeping infant. Then she hummed a single note from the page.

The candle on the altar flared.

Somewhere in the house, a dish fell from a shelf.

Outside, the leaves scattered as the wind shifted, erratic, syncing with each heartbeat.

Grace stopped.

She whispered Helen's name.

The air answered—not with words, but with warmth. A presence.

Grace exhaled and closed her eyes. Something deep beneath her skin began to stir.

She was being imprinted.

CHAPTER 2: THE LOST HYMN

The morning after the song first escaped her lips, Grace woke with the taste of iron on her tongue and a faint red stain on her hands. The house lay unusually still. Even the birds outside sang softer, as if they knew something delicate had crossed into the world and was learning how to breathe within it.

On the altar, the rosemary had dried overnight, its edges curled like an ancient scripture left open too long. She had not intended to sing. The melody had torn itself from her, the way water breaks through cracked clay—inevitable, unsought, already alive.

Downstairs, Charisse was already at the stove, frying bakes in cast iron. Grace moved quietly, the soles of her feet brushing against the floorboards, which groaned as if they remembered her childhood.

"You slept?" Charisse asked.

"Enough."

"You talk in your sleep now."

"What did I say?"

"You weren't speaking; you were humming. Sounded like a grim dirge, but not one I know."

Grace hesitated. "It's from Helen's book—the one Grandma left."

Charisse's hand froze in midair. Oil sizzled and popped around the dough, but her focus stayed fixed on Grace.

"You've been reading it?"

"I didn't plan to. It found me."

"You do not read that book like a newspaper," Charisse said. "It's for remembering. And if it speaks to you, you better be ready for what it brings."

Helen had once lost her voice after Roberto disrupted a ritual. Her silence filled the house like smoke for a year—dense, ghostly, and set apart. When her voice returned, it sang only to the dead.

Grace was tracing the same path now, humming verses she didn't understand. The cost of remembering had never been cheap for this family.

Grace swallowed hard. She had come back to bury a past, not to become it.

Later that day, Grace returned to Helen's room. Sunlight slipped through the salted windows like golden threads, illuminating dust motes and dried petals scattered across the wooden floor. The book sat where she had left it, now wrapped in a swatch of indigo cloth and tied with a red ribbon—a gesture of respect or instinct she wasn't sure.

She opened it slowly.

Each page breathed, the ink dark, with a glycerin of red that looked like the numbing sheen of dried blood. Notes curled like vines around strange sigils. She traced them with her fingers, feeling a pulse beneath her fingertips.

One page had no symbols, only lyrics. Or were they verses? Poems maybe? She couldn't be sure.

"When blood forgets its rhythm,

Ashes dance where a heart once beat

But recall the song from the bone and root—

What lay buried will rise to greet."

As she whispered the words, a torrent swept through the room. The curtains fluttered wildly, and the rosemary on the altar toppled from the pot, scattering fragrant shards across the floor. Her heart galloped.

This was no draft.

This was acknowledgment.

By late afternoon, she ventured into the village's old archive. It was a crumbling structure of clay walls and a corrugated roof, run by Mr. Ellis—a man older than time, it seemed, with cataract eyes and a voice that rasped like rusted hinges.

"You look like trouble," he said when Grace entered.

"I come in peace."

"That's what Helen used to say before she flipped the entire world."

Grace smiled, brushing her hands over the books that lined the chamber in a barely organized chaos. "You remember her well."

"Who could forget? She made the spirit walk backward just to listen."

"I'm looking for something," Grace said. "Old hymns. Maybe chants or dirges. Especially anything tied to healing—or the calling of the dead."

Mr. Ellis raised an eyebrow. "You done went and opened her book, eh?"

"I think it opened me."

He nodded somberly, then waved toward a dust-covered corner. "Try the red binder with the cracked spine. It has fragments. Songs the elders sang when the rivers flooded. Songs for teeth cutting through a baby's gums. Even one, they say, opens the mouth of the silent."

She dug for an hour, flipping pages faded by sun and time. In the red binder, near the middle, she found it—a hymn almost identical to Helen's.

Only this one ended differently.

> "When blood forgets its rhythm—
>
> …the mirror breaks, and you will see
>
> your name backward."

She copied it into a notebook, fingers trembling slightly.

"What does it mean?" she asked Mr. Ellis.

"Depends who you ask. Some say it's a calling song. Others say it is a warning."

Grace thanked him and withdrew; the sky now low and full of copper light.

Back at the house, she walked the perimeter before entering. Something told her the walls were listening. The soil was shifting. In Helen's garden, a patch of lavender had bloomed overnight, bright, defiant purple against the backdrop of weeds.

She remembered something Helen once told her when she was

younger than ten, right after the neighbor died.

"Life does not end when the body does. It just finds a new instrument. At least that's what my mother used to say."

At midnight, Grace sat cross-legged inside Helen's room. The altar candle flickered beside her, casting tall shadows that danced along the walls.

She began to hum the tune, repeating it subconsciously.

It started softly, unsure, like stepping onto ice. Then the melody found its footing, and she sang the full verse from the binder, ending with the line about mirrors and names.

As soon as the words left her lips, the candle flared—high and wild —then extinguished completely.

She was plunged into darkness.

And there she heard it.

A second voice.

Not echo.

Not memory.

Another voice, singing with her.

Low. Male. Wounded.

Grace followed it deeper.

In the back room, she found the source.

A shadow in the corner, shaped like a man. He was flickering, as if made of broken film.

The song spilled from his lips, slick like oil. She knew instantly: this was the soul Helen's mother had tried to bring back.

A man. His name vibrated in her mind—Roberto.

She felt it with certainty.

"My mother loved you," she whispered.

The shadow turned, and for a second—only a second—she saw his face.

Burned. Crying. Yes.

Then the walls groaned.

A whisper: "Wrong note."

Everything went black.

She woke outside, face in the dirt, fingers clenched around a stone that she didn't remember picking up. The stone bore a simple etch —the same broken spiral from the woven mat and Helen's drawing.

The blood trickled from her nose. Her throat ached.

The wind had stopped singing. Not because it had no song. Because it was waiting for her to carry it forward.

That evening, she told Charisse everything.

The ruins. Roberto. The vision. The blood.

Charisse was silent for a long time. Then she said, "Roberto is your father."

The words struck like thunder.

Grace's vision blurred. "But I thought…"

"You were born in fire," Charisse said. "He was Helen's first love; she left him. Your grandmother tried to set up a ward for Helen, but Roberto came in while she was doing her spell and was maimed when the ritual backfired. Helen lost her voice for a time, and when it came back, she couldn't stop singing to the dead."

During that time, Helen's father—a shipwright—moved the family away. She met Saint after. And then suddenly, only you returned with your grandmother and Abel.

"Why did you take me in as your own when the village shunned me?" Grace yelled.

"You are mine. But you were Helen's blood—born from a hymn. A lost note that needed to return to glory"

Grace fell to her knees.

She had never known her true father; she only knew Saint.

She had never known she was born of a song.

Now everything made sense.

Her voice. Her vision. The wind. The blood.

Why she was not allowed to stay with the family she grew up with.

She was the chorus, the reverberation, and the chant—and now a complete song.

And that song would be sung again.

CHAPTER 3: SOIL AND SPIRIT

Grace stood barefoot in Helen's garden at dawn, the hem of her skirt brushing dew-soaked basil and thyme. The air held the faint, sweet smell of tilled fertile ground, as if the Earth escorted secrets and was always on the verge of spewing them. She breathed in deeply, grounding herself, repeating the phrase Helen had once etched in her childhood notebook:

"Touch the soil and you will touch yourself."

For the first time in her life, she wanted to believe that the Earth knew her better than anyone else ever could.

Grace found a letter—and a hidden book—in Helen's Sanctuary, and it changed everything. Since reading it, Grace hadn't spoken to Charisse or returned to the market. She stayed near the house, near Helen's altar, listening.

The smaller book was older than the first, hand-bound with straps of coir and sinew, its pages thick and stained with oil, ash, and something reddish-brown that might have been blood. No page numbers. No order. Just entries.

Some were prayers. Others were diagrams. Some looked like recipes written in code.

She spent two days trying to make sense of it.

Then, at midnight, the wind whispered again.

"You need someone who remembers more than you."

❋   ❋   ❋

By morning, she knew exactly who that was: Mama Laranda.

Mama Laranda was ninety-four, if the stories were true—she had been delivering babies, speaking to spirits, and fighting shadows longer than most people have been alive. She lived at the edge of the forest, in a crooked house wrapped in vines, where the sun rarely broke through the canopy.

Mama Laranda, who had remained cautious around Helen, once called her "the one who danced too close to the sea's shadows."

But even she had bowed the day she found out Helen had passed, whispering a song no one else knew. Grace now walked the same edges, barefooted and bold. The forest responded like it had been waiting. For her, for the hymn, for the return.

Charisse had forbidden Grace to visit her.

"She doesn't deal in answers. Only debts," Charisse warned. "You go to her, you best be ready to pay."

But Grace was beyond fear now. The hymn lived inside of her. It demanded direction, or it would destroy her with its weight.

The forest path was thinner than Grace remembered, half-swallowed by creeping vines with overgrown audacity. Birds called from above, unseen. She carried nothing but Helen's second book wrapped in cloth and a pouch of Salara bread tied to her belt.

The deeper she walked, the more her skin itched, not with rash or sweat, but with recognition. The forest was alive. Not just in the way of birds and insects. But with memory and resonance. Every leaf, every stone, every shadow seemed to turn slightly toward her. Even the vines were waving toward her, signaling for her to hurry.

It took an hour to find the house. It leaned against a breadfruit tree, with its roof missing two corners, wind chimes made of bones and glass singing in silence.

The door creaked open before she knocked.

Inside was darkness. But not emptiness.

"Come in, Helen's echo," a raspy voice sounded from somewhere inside. "You took your time getting in here."

Grace stepped in vigilantly. The scent hit her first: cloves, cinnamon, molasses, and cayenne, followed by warmth—unlike her grandmother's house. The room was dim, lit only by red candles in coconut husks. At the center sat Mama Laranda, hair wrapped high in a golden cloth, her eyes white with glaucoma but shining as if the stars were living in them.

"You bring the book?"

Grace nodded, handing it over.

"Don't speak. Just sit."

She obeyed, settling on a red mat woven in spiral patterns.

Mama Laranda opened the book and ran her fingers across the pages, though her eyes barely moved.

"She left you the hymn. Foolish and bold." She chuckled. "Helen always danced too close to the edge."

"What is it?" Grace asked softly.

"It's not one song. It's a braid of three spirits. One is for remembering. Another is for healing. The last is for…" Her voice trailed off, "returning."

"Returning what?"

Mama Laranda stared into the candle flame. "Sometimes souls don't leave cleanly. They tangle in this world. The hymn untangled them—to bring them back to finish what they couldn't."

Grace shivered. "Is that what she did? Bring someone back?"

"She didn't. But someone did. Which caused her tide to end early. Now it is your turn."

The room went still.

"But you can't sing that hymn raw," Mama Laranda continued, "Preparation is necessary… or your memory will be its meal."

"How do I prepare?"

"Ritual. Root. Reflection."

She motioned to the side room.

"In there, you will bathe in clay, fast for a day, then we will go to the hillside of the ancestors. If they accept you, the hymn will fully reveal itself."

Grace did not hesitate.

Inside the room, a bowl of orchard clay sat beside a copper basin filled with river water. A clean cloth, dried calabash, and herbs lay folded nearby. She undressed, feeling the air on her skin like a question. With slow, revenant hands, she began coating her body in clay, from her shoulders down to the soles of her feet. It was cold at first, but the moment it dried, it warmed like sunlight.

She felt everything: her doubt, her grief, her questions sinking into the clay. It didn't just cover her; it engulfed her.

Then she sat.

She didn't sleep that night. She breathed. She listened. And just before dawn, she dreamed.

In the dream, she stood in a circle of women dressed in blue. None had faces. They each held a mirror. One by one, they turned them to Grace, and in each mirror, she saw a different version of herself: laughing, old, angry, barefoot and bleeding, giving birth, praying, dancing, dead.

Then, one step forward.

"Name yourself," she said.

Grace opened her mouth, but no sound came out. She woke with a gasp.

Mama Laranda stood over her. "You are ready."

❋ ❋ ❋

The walk to the ancestral hill was long, hot, and rhythmic. Grace felt tension in her legs, in her breath. Mama Laranda moved with the ease of a woman who had never forgotten where the ground began.

They passed termite mounds shaped like altars, and trees carved with unreadable glyphs. Somewhere overhead, vultures circled. Somewhere ahead the ancestors waited.

At the top of the hill, seven stones sat in a circle, each marked with a unique symbol: a root, a flame, a drop of blood, a drum, a mask, a star, a song.

Grace knelt before the song stone.

Mama Laranda placed the book beside her.

Grace looked up and asked, "Why are you helping me so much? I have nothing to offer."

Mama Laranda replied, "Your mother has already paid your debt. Now touch the stone and close your eyes."

As she did, the wind stilled.

Then voices, soft at first but rising, came. A thunder of sound, language, and melody braided together. The hymn was complete.

She was acknowledged.

CHAPTER 4: WHERE THE WIND SPIRIT STOPPED SINGING

Charisse didn't speak until they were both seated at the kitchen table. A single kerosene lamp burned low, casting wide shadows on the faded walls. The sound of the night insects outside was thick and alive, as though the terrain refused to be soothed.

Grace waited.

She could feel the memory of her mother rising in her chest like water against an old dam.

"I was seventeen," Charisse began, her voice flat but measured. "Helen had just turned nineteen. She came back from St. Jorge's with eyes too bright and a silence too wide. That's when the dreams started."

Grace leaned in. "What dreams?"

"Her voice was gone. Not in the day, but at night. She had screamed, but no sound escaped her vocal cords. She said someone was standing over her, singing in reverse, backward Patwa mixed with ancient English. She said they were trying to stitch her skin into a new name."

Grace's breath got caught in her chest.

Charisse went on, slowly now, unraveling the tapestry she'd hidden for decades.

"At first, her mother thought it was stress. Then we found her one morning covered in symbols, drawn in ash on her stomach and feet. Helen swore she didn't do it. She said the hymn did it. That it was waking inside her. That it needed someone to finish it."

Grace's fingers trembled under the table. "Why didn't you tell me?"

"Because I watched what it did to her, and didn't want the same for you. I watched people turn on her. They said she brought sickness. That her song twisted crops. Even after she healed a child, they said she'd caused the illness to prove her power. I did not want you to carry the same burden."

"But I already am," Grace said. "And it is heavier now because I never knew."

Charisse stood, pacing towards the cupboard. She pulled down a small metal tin can and returned to the table. Inside were old letters, fading photos, a folded piece of blue cloth, and a locks of Helen's hair, wrapped in a white and red ribbon.

"I kept it all," Charisse whispered. "Not because I believe in it. But because part of me knew I would need it for you."

She handed Grace the folded cloth.

Inside was a drawing—charcoal and water stains. It showed a woman, bare-chested, eyes hollowed, standing in a circle of fire. Around her feet were leaves. In her hands, she held a broken spiral stone and a mirror.

Grace turned it over.

Helen's handwriting sprawled across the back.

"One voice to remember.

One voice to heal.

One voice to return what must never be forgotten."

* * *

That night, Grace sat by the altar and lit the cedar. Helen's small book lay open before her, but the pages seemed to shift as though the ink was still wet.

The visions came before her eyes even closed.

She was back in the field, in the circle of women. Only this time they had faces. They were women from her lineage. All of them. Every matriarch. Her grandmother. Helen. A woman she didn't recognize but looked like a younger Charisse. In the center stood a girl no older than nine.

The child was singing.

But no sound came.

Only leaves moved in time with her mouth.

Grace stepped forward and asked, "What is her name?"

Helen answered from behind, "That's your voice, before it was silenced."

Grace began to cry.

She shouted furiously, "I want it back."

Someone replied, "Then find where the wind spirit stopped singing."

❋ ❋ ❋

The next morning, Grace knew what she had to do—where she had to go.

The old estate lands.

A mile before the river's mouth stood the ruins of a colonial house, long abandoned, sinking into itself, wrapped in poison ivy and moss. It was the place children dared each other to run past, but no one dared enter. Grace had heard from Helen that every curse-note in the land could be traced back to that place.

"You can't sing your name into the wind if you don't know where the silence began."

Grace hadn't understood it then, but she did now.

She prepared a small satchel: the hymn book, rosemary sprigs, the folded drawing, and Mama Laranda's pouch of Frankincense and Myrrh. She wore white, wrapped her hair in a blue cloth, and tied her wrist with thread soaked in seawater. Helen had once told her it was for protection rites from the sea but disguised it as a children's game.

The tide ceased singing the day they buried Helen. That's what Charisse had whispered when she lit the cedar, hands shaking. Now, with every step Grace took toward the old estate, she heard that hush stirring again. The silence wasn't emptiness. It was memory, waiting for the right voice to call it home.

She kept Charisse in the dark about her destination. A grown woman needs no one's permission.

The walk took two hours through the wild terrain. At one point, she thought she saw something watching her from the trees, a blur, not quite an animal, not quite a man. But when she turned to face it, the wind shifted, and it was gone.

At the estate's edge, vines hung low like arms reaching down. The building had collapsed on its left side, revealing blackened beams and stone carved with strange symbols older than the plantation farms that once stood there.

Grace stared at the threshold and whispered, "I am here."

Nothing answered. But the silence felt changed, alive. She stepped inside.

The air was cold. Too cold for the area. The kind of cold that didn't come from the weather but from forgetting.

She moved slowly, letting the hymn begin in her mind.

A soft hum.

The first note.

Then the second.

The third felt like a key turning an invisible lock.

Suddenly, the air changed.

A gust of wind knocked her backward, and the door slammed shut. Darkness filled the room. But a single voice, not hers, began to sing.

It shifted to her left ear, then gave a giggle on her right.

Warmth filled her. You finally found me.

CHAPTER 5: NAMES THAT WEREN'T GIVEN

The next morning, Grace walked into the village square with Helen's hymn book under her arm and the wind swirling around her ankles like a loyal dog.

Eyes followed her. Conversations paused. A goat tied to a post bleated once, then fell silent.

She was no longer the girl who ran from this place.

She was something else now, a woman stitched with wind and song, holding pieces of her own story that even the elders had buried too deep.

At the crossroads where the old mango tree grew, the village council gathered. Five men, three women. All gray-haired, stiff-spine, dressed in cream and navy. They hadn't called for her. But she knew they were waiting.

"You summoned the wind again," said Elder Mario, his tongue flat. "The dogs howled. The trees bent, my wife lost her breath."

Grace didn't flinch. "The hymn, the wind—no, my voice was never meant to be buried."

A murmur rippled through them. Elder Maria stepped forward, her gold earrings swaying.

"Helen tried to bring back a man who was taken, and she paid the price. What makes you think you won't?"

"I've already paid the price," Grace said. "In silence. In shadows. In every lie I inherited."

She laid the book down in the center of the circle.

"Read it," she said. "...or burn it, but don't pretend it didn't protect this village more times than you can admit."

Maria's lips twitched. "Words have power, but so does forgetting."

"And forgetting is why we keep bleeding the same blood," Grace said. "Why the same mother buries the same sons with the same unsung songs in their throats."

She stepped closer.

"I know who I am now. I know who my mother really was. I know the truth about Roberto. And I know the hymn isn't done."

These were the same elders who watched as Helen salted to earth after her grandmother died. The same ones who turned their backs when she healed the boy's lung with smoked lime. Grace stared into their eyes and saw the fear hadn't changed—it only aged. But she had not come to repeat Helen's silence. She came to shout it from the rooftops.

Elder Mario's gaze hardened. "You dare speak that name."

"He was my father," she replied.

Silence fell like a drop drum.

"You carried the same cursed blood," he said. "Fire-blood."

Grace replied with a smile and said, "Then let it burn."

✳ ✳ ✳

The confrontation ripped through the village like a storm cloud. By dusk, three different stories had spread.

Grace cursed the council.

Grace opened Helen's tomb.

Grace was the "new singer of the dead."

Children peeked from behind their mothers' skirts where she passed. The elders turned their backs, but the young ones, those closer to the soil than to tradition, watched with white eyes, waiting.

Charisse didn't speak a word when Grace came home.

She simply lit a lamp, pulled the curtain shut, and began to heat ginger and guava leaf in an old enamel pot.

"You should leave soon," she said, her back to Grace.

"You don't belong here anymore."

"I belong here now more than I ever did."

Her eyes were wet, but her jaw was steel.

"Do you think they'll let you finish what Helen's mother started? You think they'll let a child born in fire lead them into the light, which was cursed by the shadow?"

Grace stepped forward, reaching for Charisse's hand. "They still think it was my mother, poor lost souls. Besides, I don't need them to let me sing. I just need to."

❋ ❋ ❋

That night, she returned to Helen's room, but something had shifted. The air felt cracked—the altar was colder than usual—the cedar smoke curled in odd directions, not spiraling, but unraveling.

The vision came quickly this time, unprovoked.

She stood on a hill overlooking the village. It was nice, the sky glowing with red light.

Beneath her feet, the Earth trembled.

A voice rose, not hers, but from the soil itself.

It spoke fragments:

"You are not the first... you are the seed and the fire.

The roots remember... But the fire tests the memory."

She saw an old woman in chains. A drum burning in a pit. A child's mouth sewn shut. Then she saw Helen, younger, terrified, covered in ash in a salted circle.

And herself, barefoot, bleeding, holding a broken stone spiral of flame.

She screamed.

And woke with smoke in her throat.

* * *

At dawn, she went to Mama Laranda.

Mama Laranda was already outside, brewing something over the fire. Her eyes, despite her failing vision, flickered toward Grace as if they saw clearer than ever.

"You gone and soaked the root," she said. Grace sat beside her in silence.

"Fire ain't evil," Mama Laranda murmured. "It's just impatience."

"I saw Helen. And others. The Earth was shaking."

"Because your voice went deep."

Grace looked down. "They said I carry cursed blood."

"Good," Mama Laranda smiled. "Cursed blood is sacred blood that someone tried to shame."

She stirred her pot.

"Are you ready for the next ritual?"

Grace nodded.

"This one is not in a book. Not written in any ink. It's carried mouth to mouth, dream to dream. You gonna chant for the dead. But not just any dead—to unremembered ones."

Grace's heart pounded.

"Why?"

"Because the hymn needs all its verses. And some of them ain't been sung in generations."

* * *

That night, Mama Laranda led her deep into the forest, past a tree shaped like a twisted womb and a creek that sang in two tones.

They reached a circle of stone and bone, a forgotten, unmarked graveyard.

"Many buried here were denied names. Slaves. Stillborns. Castaways. You sing for them, and they will lend you their notes."

Mama Laranda handed her a bowl.

Inside: herbs, ash, and salt.

"Rub this on your throat. Then kneel."

Grace did.

Then chant.

At first, nothing.

Then, the ground pulsed.

A wind rose.

And voices came.

So many voices.

She couldn't separate them.

She couldn't control them.

They poured into her, not as pain, but as song.

Notes wrapped around her spine.

Drums beat inside her ribs.

A vibration settled deep in her womb.

She collapsed.

But she kept singing.

Even after her voice cracked.

Even after blood ran from her nose.

Even after the stars blurred.

When she finally stopped, hours had passed.

Mama Laranda helped her up.

"Now," she said, "you have all the verses."

Grace wept.

Not from sorrow.

But from knowing the hymn was complete.

And the fire was no longer beneath the root.

It had entered her.

The ancestors did not reject her. They had joined her voice.

She was no longer singing alone.

CHAPTER 6: RIVERS OF BONES

The river was not on any maps.

Even Mama Laranda, who knew every tree, stone, and spirit between the hills, had only ever referred to it as "The place where voices sank." Grace heard whispers while growing up, of a sacred bend in the forest on the opposite end of the river, where no one fished, where even animals went silent. It's said the river carried bones that had never been buried, where the dead hummed, instead of rested.

Now she was walking straight toward it.

Her satchel was light. A clay jar of Helen's hair, the complete hymn, and a white stone she had found pressed against her door that morning, marked with the same broken stone spiral that haunted her visions.

The path grew narrower with every step. Vines tugged at her ankles like cautious hands. The trees leaned in closer, and the air smelled of iron, mangroves, and old grief.

She wasn't afraid.

She had become.

* * *

By mid-morning, Grace reached a clearing unlike any she'd ever seen. It held a hush not of silence, but of suspended breath. The river ahead was narrow and black, not from mud, but from the unknown. No birds flew above it. No crickets chirped. The water moved without sound, like silk pulled beneath glass.

In the center of the bank was a flat stone altar, half-swallowed by roots. Etched into its face were symbols, some familiar, others shifting before her eyes like living script. Her skin prickled. The estuary wasn't just a resting place. It was a memory, woven into the land and sea.

She knelt.

Helen's hair was warm in her palm. They pulsed, as if still alive.

Grace had come not to grieve—but to release—and to ask.

Helen once told Grace, "Don't bury me where the dirt doesn't move—I need water to remember me." Grace had laughed then, thinking it superstition. But now, as some of Helen's hair slipped into the estuary, she felt the truth. Helen wasn't made for graves. She was made for song, rivers, and flowing.

She took the hymn book, opened it to the final pages, and began to hum.

The melody was new.

And ancient.

And hers.

Wind lifted from the trees and curled around her voice, carrying it out across the river like incense. The black water rippled. Then steamed.

A shape rose from it, not a body, not quite, but bones strung together with light. Female. Tall. Dreadlocked. The figure stepped toward her, dripping as if the water were made of stardust and shadow.

Helen. Or what Helen had become.

"You called out to me, my daughter," she said.

Grace's lips trembled. "I didn't mean to mother. I came to understand."

"You can't understand what you haven't released."

Grace wept.

"I don't know where to lay you down."

Helen nodded toward the sea.

"I was never meant to be buried—I wasn't meant for land. I was meant to flow."

Grace stood, opened the clay jar, and poured Helen's hair into the water.

They didn't sink.

They sang.

Every grain shimmered with song—notes Grace had never written and never heard, but recognized.

And as the verses disappeared into the water, so did Helen's hair, dissolving into light, into sound, into peace.

But the hymn didn't stop.

It spread.

From the surface of the estuary, a glow unfurled, not blinding, but soft and golden. Figures began to emerge from the water. Not fully formed, not frightening, just outlines, shimmers, fragments of memories.

A woman cradling an invisible child.

A man beating a silent bagpipe.

A girl dancing in loops, her feet tracing the shape of infinity.

They were the forgotten ones. The unnamed.

The unprayed for.

And now, they had been remembered.

The air thickened with presence. Grace spoke names she had only ever known as echoes living in her ears. Hands, made of light and dust, brushed her shoulders, her cheek, her chest. She felt their blessing. Their welcome. Their release.

A wind passed through her body, and with it, a vision.

She stood on the shoulders of every woman who had come before her in her ancestral line, holding not just their pain, but their joy. And her voice? It was no longer hers alone. It was chorus.

She saw rivers made of music, women writing history in song, children learning to chant before they walked. She saw men crying at the sound of their grandmothers' names and elders bowing in reverence to hummingbirds.

And through it all, Grace stood at the center, a living note.

Grace knelt, drained but radiant. She dipped the white stone into the river, and it glowed. When she pulled it out, a new mark had appeared beside the broken stone spiral, a closed eye.

Her name was changing.

Her story was reshaping itself around her voice.

Behind her, the trees rustled.

"Your name is whole now," said a voice.

She turned. Mama Laranda stood at the edge of the woods.

Grace hadn't heard her approach.

Mama Laranda wore a long indigo robe stitched with cowrie shells, and her walking stick had fresh carvings spiraling from top to bottom.

"They will come looking for you soon," she said.

"Why?"

"Because they'll feel the shift. Some will think the sky moved. Others will think it's just wind. But a few... a few will hear the hymn."

Grace nodded, tears drying on her cheeks.

"Come," Mama Laranda said. "There's more to do. But now... they will listen."

Grace looked back once at the estuary. The water was still again. But the air vibrated with possibility. The bones had sung, and the silence had responded.

As she followed Mama Laranda into the trees, Grace felt it, not closure, but opening.

A path unfolding beneath her feet.

The ancestors were no longer behind her.

They were walking with her.

CHAPTER 7: THE ASH
AND THE ANSWER

The air in the village shifted before the first word broke dawn.

Birds stopped singing. The water in the wells tasted slightly lingering. Even the goats, usually loud and restless at dawn, lay quiet beneath the tamarind trees. Mothers were whispering prayers before lighting their fires for breakfast. The elders sat on their porches a little longer than usual, watching the horizon like it owed them something.

Something had changed.

And most knew it.

Grace returned from the river the following day just before sunrise. Her skin smelled of clay and river smoke. Her eyes shimmered with something too bright to name, too primal to ignore. She wore white again, but not the soft white of mourning. This was bone white. Lightning white. A purity that dared to carry fire.

Charisse was waiting at the gate.

She didn't speak. Just opened the door and stepped aside.

Inside, the house felt smaller, as if the walls were adjusting to who

Grace had become.

"You're different," Charisse said at last.

"I'm the same," Grace replied. "But I've remembered who I was before the forgetting."

Charisse stared. "That estuary... it's older than the Ancient Ones."

Grace smiled. "That's why I trusted it."

❋ ❋ ❋

By midday, word had spread. People spoke in circles, hushed but hurried.

The sea had whispered once through the cracks in Helen's walls. As a child, Grace thought it was just the wind. But now, after the hymn, she realized it had been waiting for its name to return. She hummed it softly at the threshold, and the village held its breath. The tide was no longer just water; it was memory. Rumors rippled through the village.

"They say the water glowed."

"She was humming. Not a tune... a command."

"The ancestors walked."

The council met in private. Elder Mario demanded an inquiry. Elder Maria suggested exile. But not all the voices agreed. A younger member, Victoria, a woman no older than Grace, stood up and said, "What if she's exactly what we prayed for... and now we're too scared to receive it?"

The silence that followed was its own kind of war.

* * *

That evening, Grace climbed the hill where three mangrove trees grew. The locals claimed that they had been planted over the graves of three witches. She placed the hymn book at the center of the roots and began to sing.

Not loudly.

Not to anyone.

But the wind carried her voice anyway.

Below the hill, candles flickered in windows. People paused over their plates. Some stood at their doors, listening.

Some cried and didn't know why.

Some knelt.

Others trembled.

One boy, maybe six or seven, wandered from his house and walked toward the hill. He sat cross-legged at the edge of the grass and watched Grace sing.

When she finished, he whispered, "My grandmother heard that song in her sleep last night."

Grace turned to him. "What's her name?"

"Anissa."

Grace smiled. "Tell Anissa she's being remembered."

The boy didn't run. He just sat beside her in silence. And when she rose to leave, he followed her all the way to the base of the hill before turning back.

❈ ❈ ❈

That night, Grace dreamed of doors.

Hundreds of them.

Some carved from bone.

Some woven from hair.

Some made of shadows, throbbing like heartbeats.

Each door bore a name. Some were familiar. Others were erased. Some weren't written in words but in sounds, lullabies, death moans, birth cries. Others danced to remember, some to forget.

One door opened.

Helen stood behind it, younger than Grace had ever seen her. She was smiling.

"You're opening the doors, Grace."

"What's behind them?"

"Everything we have lost. And everything we still carry."

Helen stepped back.

"Keep singing. Even when they tell you to stop."

Then the doors began to sing.

And Grace woke up humming.

✽ ✽ ✽

The next few days brought a strange balance of reverence and resistance. Some villagers began leaving gifts at Grace's gate, herbs, prayer beads, bundles of sage, and rice. One woman left a live chicken with a red ribbon tied around its leg. Others came quietly in the evening to touch the door, whispering a name, while weeping and walking away.

But not all were drawn to her flame.

Others scowled as they passed. Children were pulled away when they reached out to wave. Two women threw salt at the ground near her path as they crossed themselves. At night, Grace heard footsteps in the yard. Once she found embers in a circle by the front porch, a charm to burn her voice away. On another morning, she awoke to find feathers nailed to her door and a dead crow in the center.

She swept it all away—then lit another candle.

And sang louder.

There were more dreams. More doors. But also, more whispers during the day. She heard them call her by names that didn't belong to her. Witch. Wanderer. Wrong-blooded. Breaker.

But she also heard songs. New ones.

Songs sung by children in play.

Songs hummed by old women while braiding hair.

Songs that repeated words from the hymn without them even realizing they were doing it.

The hymn was not just surviving.

It was multiplying.

* * *

Mama Laranda returned three days later.

"They watching you like you swallowed thunder," she said, sipping lemongrass tea from a gourd.

"I didn't swallow it," Grace replied. "I inherited it."

Mama Laranda nodded. "Then they best start learning how to walk in lightning."

She handed Grace something in a bundle wrapped in banana leaves. Inside was a bone flute, carved with the same closed-eye symbol now etched on Grace's stone.

"It's time to go beyond singing," Mama Laranda said. "It's time to command."

Grace felt the weight of the flute. It hummed faintly in her hand.

That evening, Mama Laranda helped her mark a circle around the house using chalk made of crushed bone and hibiscus ash. "They'll try to reach you with fear," she said. "But nothing can enter a circle drawn in purpose."

Grace drew symbols on the door. She saged the house, burying rosemary and cassia in every corner.

Then she waited.

* * *

That night, Grace stood at the edge of the village with the flute in her hand. The moon was high. The sky was open.

She blew once.

No sound came out.

But the trees bent.

The wind paused.

And the ancestors stirred.

She blew again.

And this time, the earth hummed.

From the west, a branch cracked. A woman stumbled out, one of the elders. She looked around in confusion, waking from sleep. Then she dropped to her knees.

Grace lowered the flute.

"What do you remember?" she asked.

"I remember... my grandmother singing by a fire. A song I never learned. Until now."

Grace nodded.

The hymn had become more than memory.

It had become prophecy of the prime.

And Grace, daughter of silence, born from ash and song, had become its voice.

CHAPTER 8: THE BLOOD THAT SANG

The tremor came at dusk.

Just a whisper at first, a gentle shudder beneath the mango trees. A vibration that could have been wind—imagination—an old house settling into itself. But by the time the sun slid behind the hills, the ground groaned like an ancient throat clearing.

The villagers froze.

Water in jugs rippled. Chickens squawked. Children clung to their mothers' dresses. Even the oldest dogs, those who never startle from thunder or the cracks of fire, lifted their heads.

It wasn't an earthquake. Not the kind that cracked walls or split hills.

It was something else.

Something archaic.

Something remembered.

* * *

Grace stood on the same hill where she had first sung beneath the mangrove trees. The hymn book lay open at her feet, but her eyes were closed. Her voice wove through the twilight like smoke—low, slow, and certain.

Each note she released came from a place deeper than her own breath. The hymn had stopped being something she remembered. It had become something that had memorized her.

The last time the ground groaned like this, Helen had collapsed on the altar, singing in Merican—a freedom tongue everyone had heard of but no one claimed to know. The village said it was madness. But Charisse had quietly packed herbs that night, just in case. Now, Grace felt that same tremor through her bones, not as a warning, but as a welcome.

She was halfway through the third verse when the ground trembled again—felt it in her bones.

A crack split the soil near the roots.

The mangrove trees shuddered.

Below the hill, villagers gathered in clusters. Some held rosaries. Others held machetes. Most held to silence. They weren't sure what they were witnessing: a return, a miracle, a madness, or the beginning of something they couldn't name.

Elder Mario arrived, flanked by two others from the council: Elder Angel and Elder Angelique. He held a staff etched with ancestral symbols, its wood worn smooth from generations of prayer.

He raised it once.

And the song stopped.

Grace opened her eyes.

"You bring unrest to the ground," Elder Mario said to Grace, his voice loud enough to reach the watchers below.

"I brought it back to memory," Grace replied.

"You sing things best left buried."

Grace stepped forward. "It's not the song that shakes the ground. It's the truth you tried to hide, smothered beneath the ground."

* * *

The silence that followed was heavy. The villagers watched, caught between fear and revelation.

Elder Mario pointed toward the crack by Grace's feet.

"You've opened a mouth. Now let's see what comes out."

The earth rumbled again. This time, a voice emerged, not Grace's. Not Elder Mario's. Not human.

It was a chorus.

Low.

Layered.

Immemorial.

The hymn responded.

The crack widened.

From it came bones, not scattered, but arranged. As if someone had buried them in ritual—and wanted them to be found.

Grace dropped to her knees.

She touched the nearest one. It vibrated beneath her palm.

She closed her eyes and sang.

And the ground answered.

Visions flooded her—slaves marched through this land, forced to work beneath these hills. A woman lashed for humming a forbidden tune. A healer burned at the stake for saving the wrong child. A child aborted and buried before they could speak their name.

Each bone held a song.

Each song held a name.

She sang them all.

When she finished, the ground closed.

Not violently.

Gently.

As if it had been waiting to exhale.

Mario's staff fell from his hand.

The villagers knelt.

Not to her.

To the earth.

To the song.

To what had always been.

* * *

Later that night, the air in the village shifted again. But this time, it felt light. The water in the jugs stilled. The animals rested.

Children slept dreamlessly.

And for the first time in generations, the ground did not groan.

It hummed.

But Grace could not rest.

She wandered the hills alone, the hymn still echoing in her chest. She carried the bone flute with her, but did not blow it. The wind around her had begun to speak in new cadences, not just through trees, but through stones.

By a small spring tucked between two breadfruit trees, she stopped. A sound rose from the earth, rhythmic and rising.

Drums.

No one stood nearby. But Grace knew what it meant. The ancestors were no longer merely listening. They were preparing.

❊ ❊ ❊

The following day, elders gathered in secret again. Some wanted to cast Grace out. Others feared her. Some insisted she be made priestess. Others said the ground's voice was not her doing.

"She opened a grave with song," said Elder Maria. "That is not healing. That is disturbance."

"She didn't open a grave," Elder Victoria countered. "She unsealed memory."

They debated until the sun went cold.

In the end, no decision was made. But the village pulse had changed. Half in reverence. Half in fear.

❊ ❊ ❊

Grace returned to the mangrove hill. This time, she brought the children.

She taught them the old verses first, the ones for planting. For storms. For safe birth.

Then, she taught them the new ones. The ones that had risen from the crack.

They learned quickly. Too quickly.

And when they sang in unison, the soil responded, not with fear. But with flowers.

Everywhere the children walked, wild dandelions bloomed.

Elder Maria watched from her porch. For the first time in years, her garden sprouted guava after three decades of barren soil.

She didn't speak of it.

But she whispered Grace's name before bed.

* * *

That evening, a woman Grace had never seen before came to her gate.

She was tall, robed in blue, eyes like ocean storms.

"You called us," she said.

"I sang," Grace replied.

The woman nodded. "And your song reached further than you know."

She gave Grace a piece of stone, smooth, marked with a spiral inside a sun. "When the time comes, you will know what to do."

"How will I know?"

"Another truth will be shown."

Then she left.

Grace stood holding the stone long after the woman was gone. It warmed in her hand.

* * *

Grace sat by the altar that night, candles flickering in waves. She sang only to herself. But the ground moved gently with each note.

When she looked out the window, the whole village shimmered, not in fire.

But in light.

The hymn had shaken the ground.

But it had also awakened it.

And Grace was no longer singing for remembrance.

She was singing for rebirth.

CHAPTER 9: THE SPIRAL UNCOILS

The stone didn't leave her hand that night.

Even as Grace slept, it stayed curled in her palm, the spiral carved into its surface pressing against her skin like a whisper she had not yet understood. She woke before dawn, heart thrumming, her breath fogging the windowpane as she peered outside. The village still lay quiet, the air thick with the kind of stillness that precedes change.

She stepped barefoot onto the porch, the wood cool beneath her. The sky had not yet brightened, and the moon hung like a pale bruise over Rayden's Ridge. Everything felt suspended, the breath of the world held in, waiting.

Then the sound came.

It was not thunder. Not wind. Not animals.

Bones.

They sang.

Low, hollow, like the moan of an ancient drum left beneath the earth. At first, Grace thought it was her imagination, a leftover echo from a dream. But the sound grew. Louder. Closer. Until she felt it vibrating in her ribs, her soles, her spine.

And then, the ground cracked.

Not a jagged, violent split. But a measured, intentional opening. Like the earth was exhaling long-festered secrets.

She didn't scream. She didn't run.

She stood.

Mama Laranda was already walking up the path, her staff glowing faintly with chalk symbols drawn the night before.

"You felt it," Grace said.

"I did," Mama Laranda replied. "The seal is breaking. The bones are rising to remind us—there wasn't only goodness buried below"

They moved together through the haze of early morning, passed doors flung wide in fear, passed villagers clutching children and rosaries, passed roosters who refused to crow. And all the while, the song of bones grew louder.

Down near the mangroves, the first spiral had formed.

Finger bones. Rib bones. Skull fragments. All rising from the dirt in perfect, humming sequence.

The hymn had not ended.

It had only been waiting.

❊ ❊ ❊

Grace stood on the mangrove hill by the ancient altar, the spiral etched into its surface pulsing in time with the ground. She placed the stone at its center, where Helen had once stood and knelt, on the same altar where sea salt, oil, and prayer had once mingled, and felt a current shoot through her. The symbols glowed like breath returned to bone. Helen had once been a daughter of salt and shadow. And now, Grace—the echo made flesh—was the voice the spiral had been waiting for. Whole. Remembered. Rising.

From the edge of the forest, masked figures emerged, draped in ash-colored robes, their faces painted white with glyphs of silence. They didn't speak. They didn't need to. Their presence was protest enough.

Mama Laranda stood at Grace's side.

"These are the Forgotten Watchers," she said. "They are not enemies. They are recorders of consequence."

"Then let them witness," Grace said.

She lifted the bone flute.

And blew.

No sound came at first.

Then the earth responded.

The altar cracked.

Light poured from the break, spiraling upward in ribbons of fire and gold. Villagers watched from a distance, their fear palpable. Some knelt. Others turned away.

Elder Mario pushed through the crowd, shouting, "You've brought judgment! You've broken the balance!"

Grace looked down at him.

"I've restored memory," she said.

The masked ones began to hum.

Their chant braided with Grace's voice, building into a resonance that shook the trees, that rattled shutters, that called every ancestor who had ever been denied a name.

Bones formed full figures now, skeletons wrapped in light, standing around the hill in perfect stillness. There was Roberto, not as a ghost—nor as a spirit. Remembrance incarnate.

Grace dropped to her knees.

"Let it be finished," she whispered.

And the spiral stone glowed.

Fire broke out near the edge of the village, a garden consumed by flame with no known spark. Children cried. Elders wailed. Some ran toward the river, others to the sea, while many fell to the ground in prayer. But at the center of it all, Grace was unmoved.

She was the eye of the storm.

She knelt, hands resting lightly on the altar, and began to sing again—this time, a verse no one had ever taught her:

> "From soil to soul, from dust to flame,
>
> we carry what they would not name.
>
> Through bone and note and echo wild,
>
> returns the song of every child."

The spiral in the earth burst into light.

The masked ones vanished.

The bones disassembled, not with violence, but with benevolence. They returned to the soil like satisfied prayers.

Mama Laranda stepped forward and laid a hand on Grace's shoulder.

"You are the Circle-keeper now," she said. "You've begun the third movement."

"What's the third?" Grace asked, voice shaking.

"Not healing. Not remembering. But guarding."

She pressed a second stone into Grace's hand. It bore the same spiral, but this time with a open eye etched in its center.

"What you've opened," Laranda whispered, "must be protected."

That night, Grace sat by the altar, her voice hoarse, her body tired but alive with knowing. The spiral-sun stone glowed gently in a bowl of salt beside the hymn book, which now seemed to pulse with its own breath.

She sang, softly, only to herself.

And the ground moved with her voice.

When she looked out the window, the village shimmered.

Not with fire.

But with light.

The hymn had shaken the ground.

But it had also awakened it.

She was no longer singing for remembrance.

She was singing for rebirth.

And for what came next.

The girl who once was a stranger to her bloodline now stood inside it.

Not a victim. Not a witness.

But a Keeper of the Circle.

Beneath the house, far beneath the soil, something else stirred.

The tide receded, not in fear, but in mourning.

Not ready—only aware.

Waiting.

Listening for the next note.

For the next singer.

For the next time the spiral would uncoil.